Magical Stories from

Fairyland

Illustrations by
Jean & Ron Henry

Stories by Jake Jackson

STAR FIRE

JH & RH

A Special Day

The fairies prepare themselves
for a special event...

*I*n the Rainbow Glen, the fairies of the Mountain
Top Castle were so excited. The Fisher King,
whose blue feathers ruled the glen, had foretold that
when a rainbow came to the lake, it would be a sign
for a very special event. With a twinkle in his eye, the
Fisher King advised all of the fairies to make themselves
ready for such an event. He conjured an enchanting
shower of fresh water for everyone to enjoy and made
the waters flow strong and warm.

All the fairies loved to bathe and sift their hands
through the soft, magical water of Fairyland. The little ones
enjoyed splashing and chasing around the older fairies who
gently pampered themselves with flowers and lotions from
the river banks and rock pools of the lake. As the fairies
washed and played and scrubbed and splashed, the misty
air created by the clouds of spray rose up in front of the
sunlight, to reveal a gorgeous rainbow.

Everyone knew that the Fisher King had foretold this
and they were full of wonder.

On the river, further preparations were being made. The story of the appearance of the rainbow swiftly spread down the rivers and the streams, so that soon every fairy was ready for something special to happen. Amongst the reeds and lilies, the swans decided that they would join the fun and, for this day only, they would allow the fairies to ride on their backs to decorate the river's edge.

A family of swans were nuzzling by the edges of the river, grazing for food, when a little fairy and her tiny friends asked for some help. With a quick smile the mother swan led her cygnets into the centre of the river. The little fairy had to tie some beautiful fairy lamps to the willows to hold back their weeping leaves so that everyone and everything in Fairyland could join in the special day.

The swans were strong, so the little fairy could hold herself steady. She and her fairy friends worked all day to light the lamps.

Everything was ready. The special day had arrived, just as the Fisher King had foretold. On the other side of Fairyland, the Castle of Dreams ruled the land. The Prince, who had just turned 18 years old, looked out of his window high above the land, and noticed the rainbow on the other side of Fairyland. He out of all the fairies knew what it meant. The Fisher King had told him many years before that when he saw the rainbow, he would know what it would mean.

The Prince had loved the Princess of the Rainbow Glen since his early years as a fledgling fairy. He knew that she loved him and he hoped that one day they would marry. As soon as he saw the rainbow, he dashed down the long curling staircase of the Castle and found the Princess of the Rainbow Glen waiting for him. She was dressed in her finest robes and he realised that she was the most beautiful Princess who had ever lived. The Princess had travelled all day to reach the Glen of Dreams.

As the Prince and Princess looked at each other, they knew they would be married on that day, and that they would stay together forever.

In the Hedgerows

At night, the fields are full of life...

In the hedges and the fields, amongst the berries and the grasses of spring, the fairies come out to look after the land. The sweet fragrance of the flowers mingles with the heavy scent of the dew to create a magic that draws the fairies to the meadows.

Under the light of the moon there is much to be done. Flowers that have been trampled on during the day are given new breath, bushes with torn branches are repaired, and blossom that has fallen to the floor is rescued and turned into magic.

Of course, with all this good work, there is so much fun and laughter that some of the little fairies look at each other and hope that one day, they might be together.

The Moon Maiden watches all of the activity
in the countryside. From her lofty view, she sees
the little fairies pulling at tangled weeds and helping
wounded creatures back to their homes. She sees that
every fairy has a role to play so that everyone is busy all
night long. The Moon Maiden has her own role of course.

She spots the fairies who long for another fairy
and matches them together. She weaves a pattern of stars
for the fairies to follow as they grow older and hopes that
they will choose to follow her pattern. Some decide to make
other choices, but others see the sense of her starry path.

For many years she has sat in the crescent of the moon
and cast her gaze at night. Once she had this choice to make
herself, but decided that she would become the Moon Maiden
and help all her fairy friends instead.

Holly and Pip had known each other for many years. Together they had cleared the paths of old leaves and kept the wheat free of black flies. One year they had rescued a poor beetle from underneath an old metal bucket where it had lain for days, unnoticed and starving. Pip had flown past the bucket several times but was always sorting out something else.

One day though, Pip had been rushing in one direction, Holly in the other, both looking behind them when they crashed into each other They fell to the ground and looked up dazed. Laughing, they picked themselves up and dusted down their clothes. At that moment, the path that the Moon Maiden had laid out for them was clear and they made a choice, without realising it, and suddenly kissed. Then they heard the tired breathing of the exhausted beetle and, much to his relief and gratitude, they lifted the bucket to let him free. Everyone lived happily ever after!

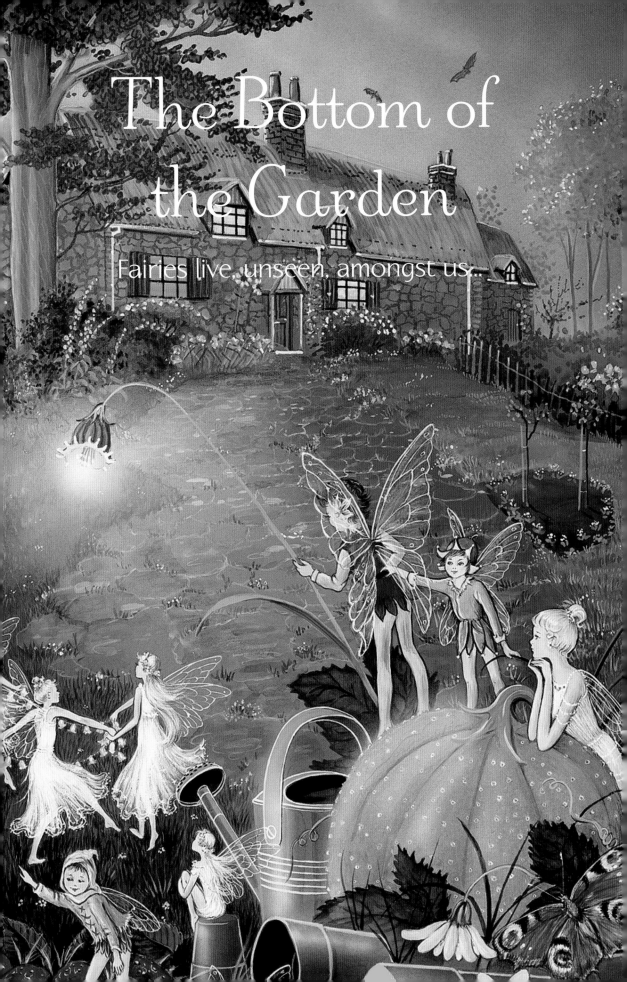

The Bottom of the Garden

Fairies live, unseen, amongst us...

*F*airies live at the bottom of every garden. As the warm lights of the cottages flicker into life, the fairies wait until they feel safe enough to venture out, for even though they cannot be seen by the human eye, there is always the chance that someone might hear their wings fluttering quietly or notice the gentle fragrance of the fairies' entrancing perfumes.

Eventually, tiny little eyes cautiously peep from the empty watering cans and flowerpots, and from underneath the berries and leaves. First one pair, then another, then a host of others appear as the fairies wake from their daytime slumbers and, stretching their delicate limbs, leap into the air.

Some bewitch the flowers to create little fairy lights, some dance to their haunting fairy tunes, and others wake up and play with their friends, the little creatures and animals.

At the end of Kitty Mae's garden is a peaceful, blue pool. A gorgeous kitten, she is used to rolling around and chasing every slight movement. During the day she races up trees and leaps across branches to the roofs of cottages. If she finds an acorn or a conker she plays for hours, chasing and pouncing and sweeping like the fastest tiger in the jungle.

At twilight though, if she hides and make sure that she is not called inside, she waits for her friends to appear. Of course, all animals can see fairies, and Kitty Mae is no exception.

The beautiful kitten is a perfect companion to the fairies, and although she is still playful, she is much more gentle at night-time than during the day. If she is really lucky the fairies play the laughing bubble game. The water nymphs blow huge bubbles from the bottom of the pool and wait for the flower fairies and Kitty Mae to catch them.

Further out into the fields, beyond the end of the garden, nestling in the hill sides and amongst the woody glades there are fairy castles. Created by old magic, the bricks and windows of the walls are all protected from the eyes of humans so that the fairies can live their lives in peace.

The fairies know that humans always rush from one place to another, never stopping to enjoy the smells and sights of the land around them. So, if you sit quietly on a hot summer's day or a cold winter's evening and stay calm for many hours, you might just see a slight shimmer in the air. If you keep still, you will notice that the air moves slightly in little pockets, darting hither and thither.

If you wait a little longer and keep ever so still, you might, out of the corner of your eye, see the gleaming turrets of a fairy castle. But you must not blink, or sneeze, or cough, or even breathe too hard. If you keep still, perhaps, just perhaps, you might see the fairies and their castles.